PERFECTION L

Baking a Cake

Vijaya Khisty Bodach

When you bake a cake, chemical changes take place. You start with

★ 1 cup shortening

★ 2 cups sugar

★ 4 eggs

★ 2 teaspoons vanilla

★ $1\frac{3}{4}$ cups milk

★ $2\frac{3}{4}$ cups flour

★ 3 teaspoons baking powder

★ 1 teaspoon salt

First you cream together
the shortening and sugar in
a bowl. Next you beat in the
eggs, vanilla, and milk.

In a separate bowl, mix the flour, baking powder, and salt.

Add the wet ingredients in the first bowl to the dry ingredients. Mix well.

Pour into a cake pan and bake at 350 degrees for 45 minutes.

The cake is done! What happened to the ingredients? Chemical changes took place and they all turned into a cake.

Picture Glossary

shortening

sugar

eggs

vanilla

milk

flour

baking powder

salt